SHARP'S GUN SERENADE

(Educate or Bust)

BY

ROBERT E. HOWARD

British Library Cataloguing-in-Publication Data
A catalogue record for this book is available from the
British Library

Robert E. Howard

Robert Ervin Howard was born in Peaster, Texas in 1906. During his youth, his family moved between a variety of Texan boomtowns, and Howard – a bookish and somewhat introverted child – was steeped in the violent myths and legends of the Old South. Although he loved reading and learning, Howard developed a distinctly Texan, hardboiled outlook on the world. He became a passionate fan of boxing, taking it up at an amateur level, and from the age of nine began to write adventure tales of semi-historical bloodshed. In 1919, when Howard was thirteen, his family moved to the Central Texas hamlet of Cross Plains, where he would stay for the rest of his life.

At fifteen Howard began to read the pulp magazines of the day, and to write more seriously. The December 1922 issue of his high school newspaper featured two of his stories, 'Golden Hope Christmas' and 'West is West'. In 1924 he sold his first piece – a short caveman tale titled 'Spear and Fang' – for $16 to the not-yet-famous *Weird Tales* magazine. He published with the magazine regularly over the next few years. 1929 was a breakout year for Howard, in that the 23-year-old writer began to sell to other magazines, such as *Ghost Stories* and *Argosy*, both of whom had previously sent him hundreds of rejection slips. In 1930, he began a correspondence with weird fiction master H. P. Lovecraft which ran up to his death six years later, and is regarded as one of the great correspondence cycles in all of fantasy literature.

It was partly due to Lovecraft's encouragement that Howard created his most famous character, Conan the Cimmerian. Conan – a barbarian-turned-King during the Hyborian Age, a mythical period of some 12,000 years ago – featured in seventeen *Weird Tales* stories between 1933 and 1936, and is now regarded as having spawned the 'sword and sorcery' genre, making Howard's influence on fantasy literature comparable to that of J. R. R. Tolkien's. The Conan stories have since been adapted many times, most famously in the series of films starring Arnold Schwarzenegger.

Howard was enjoying an all-time high in sales by the beginning of 1936, but he was also deeply upset by the ill health of his mother, who had fallen into a coma. On the morning of June 11, 1936, he asked an attending nurse whether she would ever recover, and the nurse replied negatively. Howard walked to his car, parked outside the family home in Cross Plains, and shot himself. He died eight hours later, aged just thirty.

I was heading for War Paint, jogging along easy and comfortable, when I seen a galoot coming up the trail in a cloud of dust, jest aburning the breeze. He didn't stop to pass the time of day. He went past me so fast Cap'n Kidd missed the snap he made at his hoss, which shows he was sure hightailing it. I recognized him as Jack Sprague, a young waddy which worked on a spread not far from War Paint. His face was pale and sot in a look of desprut resolution, like a man which has jest bet his pants on a pair of deuces, and he had a rope in his hand though I couldn't see nothing he might be aiming to lasso. He went fogging on up the trail into the mountains and I looked back to see if I could see the posse. Because about the only time a outlander ever heads for the high Humbolts is when he's about three jumps and a low whoop ahead of a necktie party.

I seen another cloud of dust, all right, but it warn't big enough for more'n one man, and purty soon I seen it was Bill Glanton of War Paint. But that was good enough reason for Sprague's haste, if Bill was on the prod. Glanton is from Texas, original, and whilst he is a sentimental cuss in repose he's a ring-tailed whizzer with star-spangled wheels when his feelings is ruffled. And his feelings is ruffled tolerable easy.

As soon as he seen me he yelled, "Where'd he go?"

"Who?" I says. Us Humbolt folks ain't overflowing with casual information.

"Jack Sprague!" says he. "You must of saw him. Where'd he go?"

"He didn't say," I says.

Glanton ground his teeth slightly and says, "Don't start yore derned hillbilly stallin' with me! I ain't got time to waste the week or so it takes to git information out of a Humbolt Mountain varmint. I ain't chasin' that misguided idjit to do him injury. I'm pursooin' him to save his life! A gal in War Paint has jilted him and he's so broke up about it he's threatened to ride right over the mortal ridge. Us boys has been watchin' him and follerin' him around and takin' pistols and rat-pizen and the like away from him, but this mornin' he give us the slip and taken to the hills. It was a waitress in the Bawlin' Heifer Restawrant which put me on his trail. He told her he was goin' up in the hills where he wouldn't be interfered with and hang hisself!"

"So that was why he had the rope," I says. "Well, it's his own business, ain't it?"

"No, it ain't," says Bill sternly. "When a man is in his state he ain't responsible and it's the duty of his friends to look after him. He'll thank us in the days to come. Anyway, he owes me six bucks and if he hangs hisself I'll never git paid. Come on, dang it! He'll lynch hisself whilst we stands here jawin'."

4

"Well, all right," I says. "After all, I got to think about the repertation of the Humbolts. They ain't never been a suicide committed up here before."

"Quite right," says Bill. "Nobody never got a chance to kill hisself up here, somebody else always done it for him."

BUT I IGNORED THIS SLANDER and reined Cap'n Kidd around jest as he was fixing to bite off Bill's hoss's ear. Jack had left the trail but he left sign a blind man could foller. He had a long start on us, but we both had better hosses than his'n and after awhile we come to where he'd tied his hoss amongst the bresh at the foot of Cougar Mountain. We tied our hosses too, and pushed through the bresh on foot, and right away we seen him. He was climbing up the slope toward a ledge which had a tree growing on it. One limb stuck out over the aidge and was jest right to make a swell gallows, as I told Bill.

But Bill was in a lather.

"He'll git to that ledge before we can ketch him!" says he. "What'll we do?"

"Shoot him in the laig," I suggested, but Bill says, "No, dern it! He'll bust hisself fallin' down the slope. And if we start after him he'll hustle up to that ledge and hang hisself before we can git to him. Look there, though--they's a thicket growin' up the slope west of the ledge. You circle around and crawl up through it whilst I git out in the open and attracts

5

his attention. I'll try to keep him talkin' till you can git up there and grab him from behind."

So I ducked low in the bresh and ran around the foot of the slope till I come to the thicket. Jest before I div into the tangle I seen Jack had got to the ledge and was fastening his rope to the limb which stuck out over the aidge. Then I couldn't see him no more because that thicket was so dense and full of briars it was about like crawling through a pile of fighting bobcats. But as I wormed my way up through it I heard Bill yell, "Hey, Jack, don't do that, you dern fool!"

"Lemme alone!" Jack hollered. "Don't come no closer. This here is a free country! I got a right to hang myself if I wanta!"

"But it's a dam fool thing to do," wailed Bill.

"My life is rooint!" asserted Jack. "My true love has been betrayed. I'm a wilted tumble-bug--I mean tumble-weed--on the sands of Time! Destiny has slapped the Zero brand on my flank! I--"

I dunno what else he said because at that moment I stepped into something which let out a ear-splitting squall and attached itself vi'lently to my hind laig. That was jest my luck. With all the thickets they was in the Humbolts, a derned cougar had to be sleeping in that'n. And of course it had to be me which stepped on him.

Well, no cougar is a match for a Elkins in a stand-up fight, but the way to lick him (the cougar, I mean; they

6

ain't no way to lick a Elkins) is to git yore lick in before he can clinch with you. But the bresh was so thick I didn't see him till he had holt of me and I was so stuck up with them derned briars I couldn't hardly move nohow. So before I had time to do anything about it he had sunk most of his tushes and claws into me and was reching for new holts as fast as he could rake. It was old Brigamer, too, the biggest, meanest and oldest cat in the Humbolts. Cougar Mountain is named for him and he's so dang tough he ain't even scairt of Cap'n Kidd, which is plumb pizen to all cat-animals.

Before I could git old Brigamer by the neck and haul him loose from me he had clawed my clothes all to pieces and likewise lacerated my hide free and generous. In fact he made me so mad that when I did git him loose I taken him by the tail and mowed down the bresh in a fifteen foot circle around me with him, till the hair wore off of his tail and it slipped out of my hands. Old Brigamer then laigged it off down the mountain squalling fit to bust yore ear-drums. He was the maddest cougar you ever seen, but not mad enough to renew the fray. He must of recognized me.

At that moment I heard Bill yelling for help up above me so I headed up the slope, swearing loudly and bleeding freely, and crashing through them bushes like a wild bull. Evidently the time for stealth and silence was past. I busted into the open and seen Bill hopping around on the aidge of the ledge trying to git holt of Jack which was kicking like a grasshopper on the end of the rope, jest out of rech.

"Whyn't you sneak up soft and easy like I said?" howled Bill. "I was jest about to argy him out of the notion. He'd tied the rope around his neck and was standin' on the aidge, when that racket bust loose in the bresh and scairt him so bad he fell offa the ledge! Do somethin'."

"Shoot the rope in two," I suggested, but Bill said, "No, you cussed fool! He'd fall down the cliff and break his neck!"

BUT I SEEN IT WARN'T a very big tree so I went and got my arms around it and give it a heave and loosened the roots, and then kinda twisted it around so the limb that Jack was hung to was over the ledge now. I reckon I busted most of the roots in the process, jedging from the noise. Bill's eyes popped out when he seen that, and he reched up kind of dazed like and cut the rope with his bowie. Only he forgot to grab Jack before he cut it, and Jack hit the ledge with a resounding thud.

"I believe he's dead," says Bill despairingful. "I'll never git that six bucks. Look how purple he is."

"Aw," says I, biting me off a chew of terbacker, "all men which has been hung looks that way. I remember onst the Vigilantes hung Uncle Jeppard Grimes, and it taken us three hours to bring him to after we cut him down. Of course, he'd been hangin' a hour before we found him."

"Shet up and help me revive him," snarled Bill, gitting the noose off of his neck. "You seleck the damndest times to converse about the sins of yore infernal relatives--look, he's comin' too!"

Because Jack had begun to gasp and kick around, so Bill brung out a bottle and poured a snort down his gullet, and pretty soon Jack sot up and felt of his neck. His jaws wagged but didn't make no sound.

Glanton now seemed to notice my disheveled condition for the first time. "What the hell happened to you?" he ast in amazement.

"Aw, I stepped on old Brigamer," I scowled.

"Well, whyn't you hang onto him?" he demanded. "Don't you know they's a big bounty on his pelt? We could of split the dough."

"I've had a bellyfull of old Brigamer," I replied irritably. "I don't care if I never see him again. Look what he done to my best britches! If you wants that bounty, you go after it yoreself."

"And let me alone!" onexpectedly spoke up Jack, eyeing us balefully. "I'm free, white and twenty-one. I hangs myself if I wants to."

"You won't neither," says Bill sternly. "Me and yore paw is old friends and I aim to save yore wuthless life if I have to kill you to do it."

"I defies you!" squawked Jack, making a sudden dive betwixt Bill's laigs and he would of got clean away if I hadn't snagged the seat of his britches with my spur. He then displayed startling ingratitude by hitting me with a rock and, whilst we was tying him up with the hanging rope, his langwidge was scandalous.

"Did you ever see sech a idjit?" demands Bill, setting on him and fanning hisself with his Stetson. "What we goin' to do with him? We cain't keep him tied up forever."

"We got to watch him clost till he gits out of the notion of killin' hisself," I says. "He can stay at our cabin for a spell."

"Ain't you got some sisters?" says Jack.

"A whole cabin-full," I says with feeling. "You cain't hardly walk without steppin' on one. Why?"

"I won't go," says he bitterly. "I don't never want to see no woman again, not even a mountain-woman. I'm a embittered man. The honey of love has turnt to tranchler pizen. Leave me to the buzzards and cougars."

"I got it," says Bill. "We'll take him on a huntin' trip way up in the high Humbolts. They's some of that country I'd like to see myself. Reckon yo're the only white man which has ever been up there, Breck--if we was to call you a white man."

"What you mean by that there remark?" I demanded heatedly. "You know damn well I h'ain't got nary a drop of Injun blood in me--hey, look out!"

I glimpsed a furry hide through the bresh, and thinking it was old Brigamer coming back, I pulled my pistols and started shooting at it, when a familiar voice yelled wrathfully, "Hey, you cut that out, dern it!"

THE NEXT INSTANT A pecooliar figger hove into view--a tall ga'nt old ranny with long hair and whiskers, with a club in his hand and a painter hide tied around his middle. Sprague's eyes bugged out and he says: "Who in the name uh God's that?"

"Another victim of feminine wiles," I says. "That's old Joshua Braxton, of Chawed Ear, the oldest and the toughest batchelor in South Nevada. I jedge that Miss Stark, the old maid schoolteacher, has renewed her matrimonical designs onto him. When she starts rollin' sheep's eyes at him he always dons that there grab and takes to the high sierras."

"It's the only way to perteck myself," snarled Joshua. "She'd marry me by force if I didn't resort to strategy. Not many folks comes up here and sech as does don't recognize me in this rig. What you varmints disturbin' my solitude for? Yore racket woke me up, over in my cave. When I seen old Brigamer high tailin' it for distant parts I figgered Elkins was on the mountain."

"We're here to save this young idjit from his own folly," says Bill. "You come up here because a woman wants to marry you. Jack comes up here to decorate a oak limb with his own carcass because one wouldn't marry him."

"Some men never knows their luck," says old Joshua enviously. "Now me, I yearns to return to Chawed Ear which I've been away from for a month. But whilst that old mudhen of a Miss Stark is there I haunts the wilderness if it takes the rest of my life."

"Well, be at ease, Josh," says Bill. "Miss Stark ain't there no more. She pulled out for Arizona three weeks ago."

"Halleloojah!" says Joshua, throwing away his club. "Now I can return and take my place among men--Hold on!" says he, reching for his club again, "likely they'll be gittin' some other old harridan to take her place. That new-fangled schoolhouse they got at Chawed Ear is a curse and a blight. We'll never be shet of husband-huntin' 'rithmetic shooters. I better stay up here after all."

"Don't worry," says Bill. "I seen a pitcher of the gal that's comin' from the East to take Miss Stark's place and I can assure you that a gal as young and pretty as her wouldn't never try to slap her brand on no old buzzard like you."

"Young and purty you says?" I ast with sudden interest.

"As a racin' filly!" he declared. "First time I ever knowed a school-marm could be less'n forty and have a face that

12

didn't look like the beginnin's of a long drouth. She's due into Chawed Ear on the evenin' stage, and the whole town turns out to welcome her. The mayor aims to make a speech if he's sober enough, and they've got up a band to play."

"Damn foolishness!" snorted Joshua. "I don't take no stock in eddication."

"I dunno," says I. That was before I got educated. "They's times when I wisht I could read and write. We ain't never had no school on Bear Creek."

"What would you read outside of the labels onto whiskey bottles?" snorted old Joshua.

"Funny how a purty face changes a man's viewp'int," remarked Bill. "I remember onst Miss Stark ast you how you folks up on Bear Creek would like for her to come up there and teach yore chillern, and you taken one look at her face and told her it was agen the principles of Bear Creek to have their peaceful innercence invaded by the corruptin' influences of education. You said the folks was all banded together to resist sech corruption to the last drop of blood."

"It's my duty to Bear Creek to pervide culture for the risin' generation," says I, ignoring them slanderous remarks. "I feels the urge for knowledge a-heavin' and a-surgin' in my boozum. We're goin' to have a school on Bear Creek, by golly, if I have to lick every old mossback in the Humbolts. I'll build a cabin for the schoolhouse myself."

"Where'll you git a teacher?" ast Joshua. "Chawed Ear ain't goin' to let you have their'n."

"Chawed Ear is, too," I says. "If they won't give her up peaceful I resorts to force. Bear Creek is goin' to have culture if I have to wade fetlock deep in gore to pervide it. Le's go! I'm r'arin' to open the ball for arts and letters. Air you-all with me?"

"No!" says Jack, plenty emphatic.

"What we goin' to do with him?" demands Glanton.

"Aw," I said, "we'll tie him up some place along the road and pick him up as we come back by."

"All right," says Bill, ignoring Jack's impassioned protests. "I jest as soon. My nerves is frayed ridin' herd on this young idjit and I needs a little excitement to quiet 'em. You can always be counted on for that. Anyway, I'd like to see that there school-marm gal myself. How about you, Joshua?"

"YO'RE BOTH CRAZY," growls Joshua. "But I've lived up here on nuts and jackrabbits till I ain't shore of my own sanity. Anyway, I know the only way to disagree successfully with Elkins is to kill him, and I got strong doubts of bein' able to do that. Lead on! I'll do anything within reason to help keep eddication out of Chawed Ear. T'ain't only my personal feelin's regardin' schoolteachers. It's the principle of the thing."

"Git yore clothes and le's hustle then," I says.

"This painter hide is all I got," says he.

"You cain't go down into the settlements in that rig," I says.

"I can and will," says he. "I look as civilized as you do, with yore clothes all tore to rags account of old Brigamer. I got a hoss clost by. I'll git him if old Brigamer ain't already."

So Joshua went to git his hoss and me and Bill toted Jack down the slope to where our hosses was. His conversation was plentiful and heated, but we ignored it, and was jest tying him onto his hoss when Joshua arrov with his critter. Then the trouble started. Cap'n Kidd evidently thought Joshua was some kind of a varmint because every time Joshua come nigh him he taken in after him and run him up a tree. And every time Joshua tried to come down, Cap'n Kidd busted loose from me and run him back up again.

I didn't git no help from Bill. All he done was laugh like a spotted hyener till Cap'n Kidd got irritated at them guffaws and kicked him in the belly and knocked him clean through a clump of spruces. Time I got him ontangled he looked about as disreputable as what I did because most of his clothes was tore off of him. We couldn't find his hat, neither, so I tore up what was left of my shirt and he tied the pieces around his head, like a Apache. Exceptin' Jack, we was sure a wild-looking bunch.

But I was disgusted thinking about how much time we was wasting whilst all the time Bear Creek was wallering in ignorance, so the next time Cap'n Kidd went for Joshua I took and busted him betwixt the ears with my six-shooter and that had some effect onto him--a little.

So we sot out, with Jack tied onto his hoss and cussing something terrible, and Joshua on a ga'nt old nag he rode bareback with a hackamore. I had Bill to ride betwixt him and me so's to keep that painter hide as far away from Cap'n Kidd as possible, but every time the wind shifted and blowed the smell to him, Cap'n Kidd reched over and taken a bite at Joshua, and sometimes he bit Bill's hoss by accident, and sometimes he bit Bill, and the langwidge Bill directed at that pore animal was shocking to hear.

We was aiming for the trail that runs down from Bear Creek into the Chawed Ear road, and we hit it a mile west of Bowie Knife Pass. We left Jack tied to a nice shady oak tree in the pass and told him we'd be back for him in a few hours, but some folks is never satisfied. 'Stead of being grateful for all the trouble we'd went to for him, he acted right nasty and called us some names I wouldn't of endured if he'd been in his right mind.

But we tied his hoss to the same tree and hustled down the trail and presently come out onto the War Paint-Chawed Ear road, some miles west of Chawed Ear. And there we sighted our first human--a feller on a pinto mare and when he seen us he give a shriek and took out down the road toward Chawed Ear like the devil had him by the britches.

"Le's ast him if the teacher's got there yet," I suggested, so we taken out after him, yelling for him to wait a minute. But he jest spurred his hoss that much harder and before we'd gone any piece, Joshua's fool hoss jostled agen Cap'n Kidd, which smelt that painter skin and got the bit betwixt his teeth and run Joshua and his hoss three miles through the bresh before I could stop him. Bill follered us, and of course, time we got back to the road, the feller on the pinto mare was out of sight long ago.

SO WE HEADED FOR CHAWED Ear but everybody that lived along the road had run into their cabins and bolted the doors, and they shot at us through the winders as we rode by. Bill said irritably, after having his off-ear nicked by a buffalo rifle, he says, "Dern it, they must know we aim to steal their schoolteacher."

"Aw, they couldn't know that," I says. "I bet they is a war on betwixt Chawed Ear and War Paint."

"Well, what they shootin' at me for, then?" demanded Joshua.

"How could they recognize you in that rig?" I ast. "What's that?"

Ahead of us, away down the road, we seen a cloud of dust, and here come a gang of men on hosses, waving guns and yelling.

"Well, whatever the reason is," says Bill, "we better not stop to find out! Them gents is out for blood, and," says he

17

as the bullets begun to knock up the dust around us, "I jedge it's our blood!"

"Pull into the bresh," says I. "I goes to Chawed Ear in spite of hell, high water and all the gunmen they can raise."

So we taken to the bresh, and they lit in after us, about forty or fifty of 'em, but we dodged and circled and taken short cuts old Joshua knowed about, and when we emerged into the town of Chawed Ear, our pursewers warn't nowheres in sight. In fack, they warn't nobody in sight. All the doors was closed and the shutters up on the cabins and saloons and stores and everything. It was pecooliar.

As we rode into the clearing somebody let bam at us with a shotgun from the nearest cabin, and the load combed Joshua's whiskers. This made me mad, so I rode at the cabin and pulled my foot out'n the stirrup and kicked the door in, and whilst I was doing this, the feller inside hollered and jumped out the winder, and Bill grabbed him by the neck. It was Esau Barlow, one of Chawed Ear's confirmed citizens.

"What the hell's the matter with you buzzards?" roared Bill.

"Is that you, Glanton?" gasped Esau, blinking his eyes.

"A-course it's me!" roared Bill. "Do I look like a Injun?"

"Yes?ow! I mean, I didn't know you in that there turban," says Esau. "Am I dreamin' or is that Josh Braxton and Breck Elkins?"

18

"Shore it's us," snorted Joshua. "Who you think?"

"Well," says Esau, rubbing his neck and looking sidewise at Joshua's painter skin. "I didn't know!"

"Where is everybody?" Joshua demanded.

"Well," says Esau, "a little while ago Dick Lynch rode into town with his hoss all of a lather and swore he'd jest outrun the wildest war-party that ever come down from the hills!"

"'Boys,' says Dick, 'they ain't neither Injuns nor white men! They're wild men, that's what! One of 'em's big as a grizzly b'ar, with no shirt on, and he's ridin' a hoss bigger'n a bull moose! One of the others is as ragged and ugly as him, but not so big, and wearin' a Apache headdress. T'other'n's got nothin' on but a painter's hide and a club and his hair and whiskers falls to his shoulders. When they seen me,' says Dick, 'they sot up awful yells and come for me like a gang of man-eatin' cannibals. I fogged it for town,' says Dick, warnin' everybody along the road to fort theirselves in their cabins."

"Well," says Esau, "when he says that, sech men as was left in town got their hosses and guns and they taken out up the road to meet the war-party before it got into town."

"Well, of all the fools!" I says. "Say, where's the new teacher?"

"The stage ain't arriv yet," says he. "The mayor and the band rode out to meet it at the Yaller Creek crossin' and escort her in to town in honor. They'd left before Dick brung news of the war-party."

"Come on!" I says to my warriors. "We likewise meets that stage!"

So we fogged it on through the town and down the road, and purty soon we heard music blaring ahead of us, and men yipping and shooting off their pistols like they does when they're celebrating, so we jedged they'd met the stage and was escorting it in.

"What you goin' to do now?" ast Bill, and about that time a noise bust out behind us and we looked back and seen that gang of Chawed Ear maniacs which had been chasing us dusting down the road after us, waving their Winchesters. I knowed they warn't no use to try to explain to them that we warn't no war-party of cannibals. They'd salivate us before we could git clost enough to make 'em hear what we was saying. So I yelled: "Come on. If they git her into town they'll fort theirselves agen us. We takes her now! Foller me!"

SO WE SWEPT DOWN THE road and around the bend and there was the stage coach coming up the road with the mayor riding alongside with his hat in his hand, and a whiskey bottle sticking out of each saddle bag and his hip pocket. He was orating at the top of his voice to make hisself heard above the racket the band was making. They was blowing horns and banging drums and twanging on Jews harps, and the hosses was skittish and shying and jumping.

But we heard the mayor say, "--And so we welcomes you, Miss Devon, to our peaceful little community where life runs smooth and tranquil and men's souls is overflowin' with milk and honey--" And jest then we stormed around the bend and come tearing down on 'em with the mob right behind us yelling and cussing and shooting free and fervent.

The next minute they was the damndest mix-up you ever seen, what with the hosses bucking their riders off, and men yelling and cussing, and the hosses hitched to the stage running away and knocking the mayor off'n his hoss. We hit 'em like a cyclone and they shot at us and hit us over the head with their music horns, and right in the middle of the fray the mob behind us rounded the bend and piled up amongst us before they could check their hosses, and everybody was so confused they started fighting everybody else. Nobody knowed what it was all about but me and my warriors. But Chawed Ear's motto is: "When in doubt, shoot!"

So they laid into us and into each other free and hearty. And we was far from idle. Old Joshua was laying out his feller-townsmen right and left with his ellum club, saving Chawed Ear from education in spite of itself, and Glanton was beating the band over their heads with his six-shooter, and I was trompling folks in my rush for the stage.

The fool hosses had whirled around and started in the general direction of the Atlantic Ocean, and the driver and the shotgun guard couldn't stop 'em. But Cap'n Kidd

21

overtook it in maybe a dozen strides and I left the saddle in a flying leap and landed on it. The guard tried to shoot me with his shotgun so I throwed it into a alder clump and he didn't let go of it quick enough so he went along with it.

I then grabbed the ribbons out of the driver's hands and swung them fool hosses around on their hind laigs, and the stage kind of revolved on one wheel for a dizzy instant, and then settled down again and we headed back up the road lickety-split and in a instant was right amongst the fracas that was going on around Bill and Joshua.

About that time I noticed that the driver was trying to stab me with a butcher knife so I kind of tossed him off the stage and there ain't no sense in him going around threatening to have me arrested account of him landing headfirst in the bass horn so it taken seven men to pull him out. He ought to watch where he falls when he gits throwed off of a stage going at a high run.

I also feels that the mayor is prone to carry petty grudges or he wouldn't be so bitter about me accidentally running over him with all four wheels. And it ain't my fault he was stepped on by Cap'n Kidd, neither. Cap'n Kidd was jest follering the stage because he knowed I was on it. And it naturally irritates him to stumble over somebody and that's why he chawed the mayor's ear.

As for them other fellers which happened to git knocked down and run over by the stage, I didn't have nothing personal agen 'em. I was jest rescuing Joshua and Bill which was outnumbered about twenty to one. I was doing them Chawed Ear idjits a favor, if they only knowed it, because in about another minute Bill would of started using the front ends of his six-shooters instead of the butts and the fight would of turnt into a massacre. Bill has got a awful temper.

Him and Joshua had did the enemy considerable damage but the battle was going agen 'em when I arriv on the field of carnage. As the stage crashed through the mob I reched down and got Joshua by the neck and pulled him out from under about fifteen men which was beating him to death with their gun butts and pulling out his whiskers by the handfulls and I slung him up on top of the other luggage. About that time we was rushing past the dogpile which Bill was the center of and I reched down and snared him as we went by, but three of the men which had holt of him wouldn't let go, so I hauled all four of 'em up onto the stage. I then handled the team with one hand and used the other'n to pull them idjits loose from Bill like pulling ticks off'n a cow's hide, and then throwed 'em at the mob which was chasing us.

MEN AND HOSSES PILED up in a stack on the road which was further messed up by Cap'n Kidd plowing through it as he come busting along after the stage, and by the time we sighted Chawed Ear again, our enemies was far behind us, though still rambunctious.

We tore through Chawed Ear in a fog of dust and the women and chillern which had ventured out of their shacks squalled and run back again, though they warn't in no danger. But Chawed Ear folks is pecooliar that way.

When we was out of sight of Chawed Ear I give the lines to Bill and swung down on the side of the stage and stuck my head in. They was one of the purtiest gals I ever seen in there, all huddled up in a corner and looking so pale and scairt I was afraid she was going to faint, which I'd heard Eastern gals has a habit of doing.

"Oh, spare me!" she begged. "Please don't scalp me!"

"Be at ease, Miss Devon," I reassured her. "I ain't no Injun, nor no wild man neither. Neither is my friends here. We wouldn't none of us hurt a flea. We're that refined and soft-hearted you wouldn't believe it--" At that instant a wheel hit a stump and the stage jumped into the air and I bit my tongue and roared in some irritation, "Bill, you condemned son of a striped polecat, stop this stage before I comes up there and breaks yore cussed neck!"

"Try, you beef headed lummox," he invites, but he pulled up the hosses and I taken off my hat and opened the door. Bill and Joshua clumb down and peered over my shoulder. Miss Devon looked tolerable sick. Maybe it was something she et.

"Miss Devon," I says, "I begs yore pardon for this here informal welcome. But you sees before you a man whose

24

heart bleeds for the benighted state of his native community.
I'm Breckinridge Elkins, of Bear Creek, where hearts is pure
and motives is lofty, but culture is weak.

"You sees before you," says I, growing more enthusiastic
about education the longer I looked at them big brown eyes
of her'n, "a man which has growed up in ignorance. I cain't
neither read nor write. Joshua here, in the painter skin, he
cain't neither, and neither can Bill"

"That's a lie," says Bill. "I can read and--ooomp!" I'd
kind of stuck my elbow in his stummick. I didn't want him
to spile the effeck of my speech. Miss Devon was gitting
some of her color back.

"Miss Devon," I says, "will you please ma'm come up to
Bear Creek and be our schoolteacher?"

"Why," says she bewilderedly, "I came West expecting
to teach at Chawed Ear, but I haven't signed any contract,
and--"

"How much was them snake-hunters goin' to pay you?"
I ast.

"Ninety dollars a month," says she.

"We pays you a hundred," I says. "Board and lodgin'
free."

"Hell's fire," says Bill. "They never was that much hard
cash money on Bear Creek."

"We all donates coon hides and corn licker," I snapped. "I sells the stuff in War Paint and hands the dough to Miss Devon. Will you keep yore snout out of my business."

"But what will the people of Chewed Ear say?" she wonders.

"Nothin'," I told her heartily. "I'll tend to them!"

"It seems so strange and irregular," says she weakly. "I don't know."

"Then it's all settled!" I says. "Great! Le's go!"

"Where?" she gasped, grabbing holt of the stage as I clumb onto the seat.

"Bear Creek!" I says. "Varmints and hoss-thieves, hunt the bresh! Culture is on her way to Bear Creek!" And we went fogging it down the road as fast as the hosses could hump it. Onst I looked back at Miss Devon and seen her getting pale again, so I yelled above the clatter of the wheels, "Don't be scairt, Miss Devon! Ain't nothin' goin' to hurt you. B. Elkins is on the job to perteck you, and I aim to be at yore side from now on!"

At this she said something I didn't understand. In fack, it sounded like a low moan. And then I heard Joshua say to Bill, hollering to make hisself heard, "Eddication my eye! The big chump's lookin' for a wife, that's what! Ten to one she gives him the mitten!"

"I takes that," bawled Bill, and I bellered, "Shet up that noise! Quit discussin' my private business so dern public! I--what's that?"

It sounded like firecrackers popping back down the road. Bill yelled, "Holy smoke, it's them Chawed Ear maniacs! They're still on our trail and they're gainin' on us!"

CUSSING HEARTILY I poured leather into them fool hosses, and jest then we hit the mouth of the Bear Creek trail and I swung into it. They'd never been a wheel on that trail before, and the going was tolerable rough. It was all Bill and Joshua could do to keep from gitting throwed off, and they was seldom more'n one wheel on the ground at a time. Naturally the mob gained on us and when we roared up into Bowie Knife Pass they warn't more'n a quarter mile behind us, whooping bodacious.

I pulled up the hosses beside the tree where Jack Sprague was still tied up to. He gawped at Miss Devon and she gawped back at him.

"Listen," I says, "here's a lady in distress which we're rescuin' from teachin' school in Chawed Ear. A mob's right behind us. This ain't no time to think about yoreself. Will you postpone yore sooicide if I turn you loose, and git onto this stage and take the young lady up the trail whilst the rest of us turns back the mob?"

"I will!" says he with more enthusiasm than he'd showed since we stopped him from hanging hisself. So I cut him loose and he clumb onto the stage.

"Drive on to Kiowa Canyon," I told him as he picked up the lines. "Wait for us there. Don't be scairt, Miss Devon! I'll soon be with you! B. Elkins never fails a lady fair!"

"Gup!" says Jack, and the stage went clattering and banging up the trail and me and Joshua and Bill taken cover amongst the big rocks that was on each side of the trail. The pass was jest a narrer gorge, and a lovely place for a ambush as I remarked.

Well, here they come howling up the steep slope yelling and spurring and shooting wild, and me and Bill give 'em a salute with our pistols. The charge halted plumb sudden. They knowed they was licked. They couldn't git at us because they couldn't climb the cliffs. So after firing a volley which damaged nothing but the atmosphere, they turnt around and hightailed it back towards Chawed Ear.

"I hope that's a lesson to 'em," says I as I riz. "Come! I cain't wait to git culture started on Bear Creek!"

"You cain't wait to git to sparkin' that gal," snorted Joshua. But I ignored him and forked Cap'n Kidd and headed up the trail, and him and Bill follered, riding double on Jack Sprague's hoss.

"Why should I deny my honorable intentions?" I says presently. "Anybody can see Miss Devon is already learnin' to love me! If Jack had my attraction for the fair sex, he wouldn't be luggin' around a ruint life. Hey, where's the stage?" Because we'd reched Kiowa Canyon and they warn't no stage.

"Here's a note stuck on a tree," says Bill. "I'll read it--well, for Lord's sake!" he yelped, "Lissen to this:

"'Dere boys: I've desided I ain't going to hang myself, and Miss Devon has desided she don't want to teach school at Bear Creek. Breck gives her the willies. She ain't altogther shore he's human. With me it's love at first site and she's scairt if she don't marry somebody Breck will marry her, and she says I'm the best looking prospeck she's saw so far. So we're heading for War Paint to git married.

Yores trooly, Jack Sprague.'"

"Aw, don't take it like that," says Bill as I give a maddened howl and impulsively commenced to rip up all the saplings in rech. "You've saved his life and brung him happiness!"

"And what have I brung me?" I yelled, tearing the limbs off a oak in a effort to relieve my feelings. "Culture on Bear Creek is shot to hell and my honest love has been betrayed! Bill Glanton, the next ranny you chase up into the Humbolts to commit sooicide he don't have to worry about gittin bumped off--I attends to it myself, personal!"

www.ingramcontent.com/pod-product-compliance
Lightning Source LLC
Chambersburg PA
CBHW030243180626
46810CB00008B/3266